Way Down Deep
in the
Deep Blue Sea

by
Jan Peck

illustrated by
Valeria Petrone

SIMON & SCHUSTER BOOKS FOR YOUNG READERS
New York London Toronto Sydney Singapore

My deepest heartfelt thanks to David R. Davis, Cerelle Woods, Melissa Russell, Kathryn Lay, Diane Roberts, BJ Stone, Janet Fick, Debra Deur, Chris Ford, Tom McDermott, Sue Ward, Deborah J. Lightfoot, Trish Holland, Amanda Jenkins, and my editor, Kevin L. Lewis—J. P.

SIMON & SCHUSTER BOOKS FOR YOUNG READERS
An imprint of Simon & Schuster Children's Publishing Division
1230 Avenue of the Americas, New York, New York 10020
Text copyright © 2004 by Jan Peck
Illustrations copyright © 2004 by Valeria Petrone
All rights reserved, including the right of reproduction in whole or in part in any form.
SIMON & SCHUSTER BOOKS FOR YOUNG READERS is a trademark of Simon & Schuster, Inc.
Book design by Gregory Stadnyk
The text for this book is set in Fink Heavy.
The illustrations for this book are rendered digitally.
Manufactured in China
18 20 19 17
Library of Congress Cataloging-in-Publication Data
Way down deep in the deep blue sea / Jan Peck ; illustrated by Valeria Petrone.–1st ed.
p. cm.
Summary: A child explores the treasures of the deep blue sea from the safety of a bathtub.
ISBN-13: 978-0-689-85110-0 (ISBN-10: 0-689-85110-3)
[1. Ocean–Fiction. 2. Marine animals–Fiction. 3. Stories in rhyme.] I. Petrone, Valeria, ill. II. Title.
PZ8.3.P2754 Way 2003
[E]–dc21   2002155867
0617 SCP

To my Four-Star Critique Group, and my editor, Kevin L. Lewis—J. P.

For Rosie and Phoebe—V. P.

Way down deep in the deep blue sea,
I'm looking for a treasure
for my mama and me.
I'm so brave,
can't scare me,
way down deep in the deep blue sea.

Way down deep in the deep blue sea,
I spy a sea horse racing by me.
Hello, sea horse.
Giddy-up, sea horse.
See you later, sea horse.

Swim away.

Way down deep in the deep blue sea,
I spy a hermit crab hiding from me.
Hello, crab.
Peek-a-boo, crab.
See you later, crab.

Swim away.

Way down deep in the deep blue sea,
I spy a starfish dancing by me.
Hello, starfish.
Do-si-do, starfish.
See you later, starfish.

Swim away.

Way down deep in the deep blue sea,
I spy a sea turtle following me.
Hello, turtle.
Tag along, turtle.
See you later, turtle.

Swim away.

Way down deep in the deep blue sea,
I spy an octopus waving at me.
Hello, octopus.
Gimme eight, octopus.
See you later, octopus.

Swim away.

Way down deep in the deep blue sea,
I spy a dolphin diving by me.
Hello, dolphin.
Hitch a ride, dolphin.
See you later, dolphin.

Swim away.

Way down deep in the deep blue sea,
I spy a swordfish fencing with me.
Hello, swordfish.
Touché, swordfish.
See you later, swordfish.

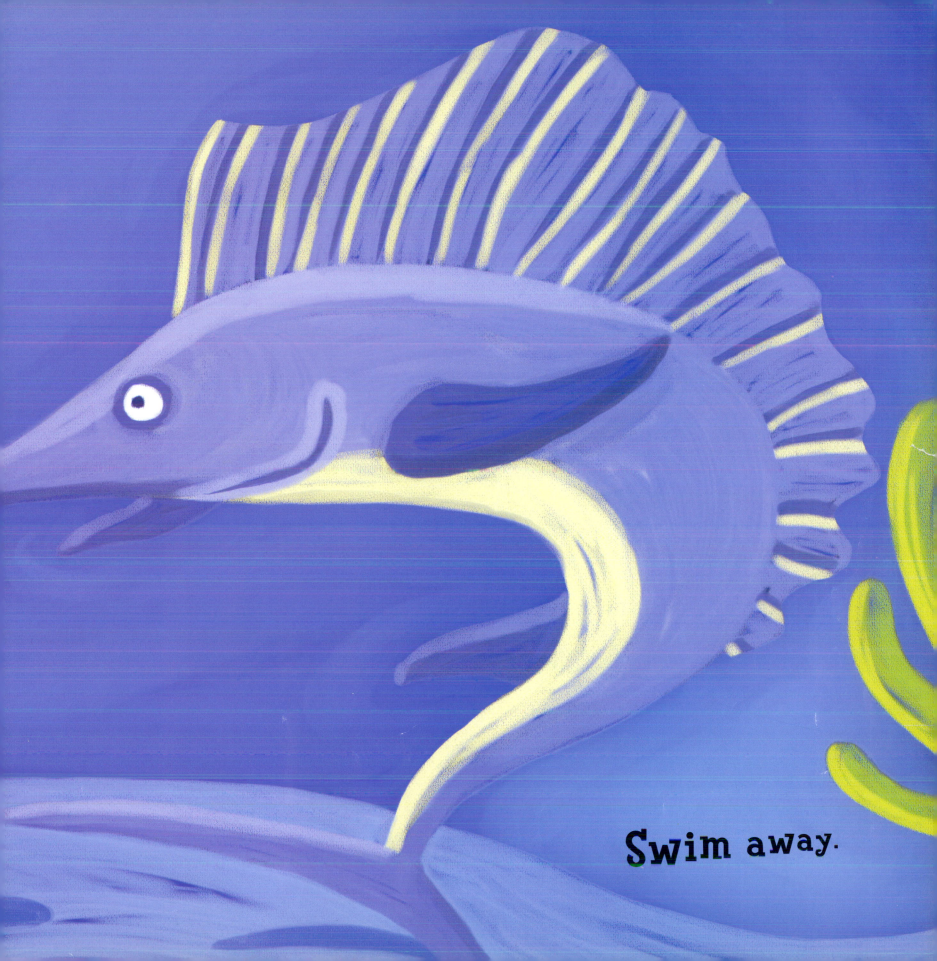

Swim away.

Way down deep in the deep blue sea,
I spy a whale spouting water by me.
Hello, whale.
Sing along, whale.
See you later, whale.

Swim away.

Way down deep in the deep blue sea,
I spy treasure gleaming at me.
Hello, treasure.
Pirate treasure.
Take-along treasure.

Swim away.

Way down deep in the deep blue sea,
I spy a shark laughing at me!

Good-bye, shark!

Good-bye, whale!
Good-bye, swordfish!
Good-bye, dolphin!

Good-bye, octopus!
Good-bye, turtle!
Good-bye, starfish!
Good-bye, hermit crab!
Good-bye, sea horse!

Up, up, up from the deep blue sea,
I find Mama waiting for me.
Hello, Mama!
Guess what, Mama?
I found treasure in the deep blue sea!